# animal house

*Especially for*

# Lauren, John,
# Allison, and Melinda

*. . . and with much thanks to Rebecca Davis, Heather Wood, and the Tuesday gang*
*for being true accomplices on this one.*

**SIMON & SCHUSTER BOOKS FOR YOUNG READERS**

An imprint of Simon & Schuster Children's Publishing Division

1230 Avenue of the Americas, New York, NY 10020

Copyright © 1999 by Melissa Bay Mathis

All rights reserved including the right of reproduction in whole or in part in any form.

SIMON & SCHUSTER BOOKS FOR YOUNG READERS

is a trademark of Simon & Schuster.

Book design by Heather Wood / The text of this book is set in Highlander.

Printed in Hong Kong

10 9 8 7 6 5 4 3 2 1

Library of Congress Cataloging-in-Publication Data

Mathis, Melissa Bay.

Animal house / Melissa Bay Mathis.—1st ed.

p. cm.

Summary: Various animals offer suggestions to make a children's treehouse a fun place to play.

0-689-81594-8 [1. Treehouses—Fiction. 2. Animals—Fiction. 3. Stories in rhyme.] I. Title.

PZ8.3.M4265Ap 1999 [E]—dc21 98-36597

**A Note from the Artist** • *The art was prepared using acrylic paints, colored pencils, and pastels. Rabbits supervised the entire operation.*

# animal house

## Melissa Bay Mathis

SIMON & SCHUSTER

BOOKS FOR YOUNG READERS

Animals know how to live!
They spend their time on fun.
They climb up trees, they roll in mud,
they dive, they leap, they run.
And when they journey home at last
to burrow, nest, or lair,
their house is made from something wild
like twigs or mud or hair. . . .

We're just like them! We want to have
a place that's made for play,
where dirt and noise are welcome—
built the animal way.
Here we have some architects
with talent, brains, and fur.
Let's ask them to help us plan
the house we'd all prefer!

"A cozy house," the otter says,
"must first of all be wet.
The center of your fun should be
the biggest bathtub yet!
Put a moat around the place,
chockful of clams and fishes.
When hunger calls, just grab a pole
and catch your favorite dishes!"

"No need for stairs or ladders.
Instead, consider these:
ropes so you can swing and sway
like we do in the trees.
Snacks could be hung high and low.
Then if you want a treat,
pick one as you glide on by—
no need to stop to eat."

"For P.J. parties, I suggest
a great big pile of hay!
It's sure to keep you toasty
while you sleep and while you play.
And don't forget the best part:
It's bedding you can munch.
You jump on it, you hide in it,
then—*voila!*—it's your lunch!"

"Have you thought of windows?
Of course you want them high,
to catch each star and rainbow
as it dances across the sky.
*Please* don't paint the ceilings white.
That's such an awful bore.
Put a fancy rug up there!
Why waste it on the floor?"

On the books: GREAT SERPENTS FROM HISTORY, KNOW YOUR DINO, REPTILE LIFE

"With your eye fixed on the blue,
I fear you'll miss the green—
for in between the grassblades
there are mysteries to be seen.
Who's that digging upward?
What's that eerie glow?
For front row seats to *this* parade
your windows should be low!"

"I see no need for windows,
but put in a hidden door.
Beds made wide and bouncy
since jumping's what they're for!
Plant the garden carefully
so when you're hopping high,
it won't be hard to pick your share
of goodies from the sky!"

"But what about the wonder
of sunlight on your fur?
Build to the sky, take off the roofs.
Now that's what makes *me* purr!
And don't forget that furniture—
each curtain, rug, and chair—
is really playground equipment
for everyone to share!"

"Let's discuss a room for snacks,"
the pig says with a squeal.
"You've got to have a floor of mud
to serve a proper meal.
A big room, too, with lots of space
for all your pals to huddle.
There's nothing as delicious as
a party in a puddle!"

"But if you want your treasures safe
and always close at hand,
besides the mud you've got to have
some nice dry dirt and sand.
We dogs suggest conveniences.
We choose the modern way:
indoor plumbing, snack dispensers,
and computer games to play!"

"The most important question
is: Do you have enough
cubbyholes and hideaways
to store all of your stuff?
I've sketched out lots of closets—
nooks of every shape and size.
If I could find that blueprint,
you could see with your own eyes!"

We've listened to each animal—
we've got our lists and plans.
It's time to build a masterpiece
with tools and paws and hands!

We said we want a treehouse, and
the grown-ups said O.K.
When it's all done, we'll ask you to . . .

We said we want a treehouse, and
the grown-ups said O.K.
When it's all done, we'll ask you to . . .

# What's YOUR idea of a perfect home?

## You've heard our ideas . . . now it's your turn!

We invite you to send us a letter and drawing showing what your dream home would be like. If your pets or stuffed animals have ideas, please translate for them and send those along, too.

Mail your letters and pictures to:

**Melissa Bay Mathis**
**c/o Simon & Schuster Books for Young Readers**
**1230 Avenue of the Americas**
**New York, NY 10020**

And visit our Web site at:
http://www.melissabaymathis.com

We look forward to hearing from you and your animals!

come on over and PLAY!

What's YOUR idea
of a perfect home?

You've heard our ideas . . .
now it's your turn!

We invite you to send us a letter and drawing
showing what your dream home would be like.
If your pets or stuffed animals have ideas,
please translate for them and send those along, too.

Mail your letters and pictures to:

**Melissa Bay Mathis**
**c/o Simon & Schuster Books for Young Readers**
**1230 Avenue of the Americas**
**New York, NY 10020**

And visit our Web site at:
http://www.melissabaymathis.com

We look
forward to
hearing from
you and
your animals!